TYPHOON

by

JAMES LOVEGROVE

The 5 Lords of Pain
Book 4

First published in 2010 in Great Britain by
Barrington Stoke Ltd
18 Walker Street, Edinburgh, EH3 7LP

www.barringtonstoke.co.uk

ISBN: 978-1-84299-816-8

Printed in Great Britain by Bell & Bain Ltd

Check out the 5 Lords of Pain
website:

www.fivelordsofpain.co.uk

For amazing downloads, behind-the-
scenes action and an exclusive
extract from the next book ...

The 5 Lords of Pain Books

Contents

The Story So Far

The Contest takes place every 30 years. It's a series of duels between five demons and a single human champion. What's at stake is nothing less than the fate of the world.

The human champion is always a member of the Yamada family. The task of defeating the demons, who are known as the Five Lords of Pain, is passed down from father to son. It has been that way for many hundreds of years.

Tom Yamada is the latest in line to face the Five Lords. Tom is only fifteen, and his Contest isn't due to start until he is 30. Something has gone wrong, however. Now Tom finds himself having to fight the duels long before he is supposed to.

Tom has won the first three duels, beating the Lord of the Mountain, the Lord of the Void, and the Lord of Tears.

He has also seen off an attack by a group of sinister zombie ninjas known as Shinobi Ghosts. A Shinobi Ghost, acting on the orders of Tom's Great-aunt Akiko, had badly hurt his best friend Sharif.

Tom wasn't so successful, however, against his own cousin, Mai. She defeated him in single combat.

Now Tom is just days away from his fourth duel, against the Lord of the Typhoon ...

Chapter 1
Camden Market

Tom Yamada had battled demons.

He'd faced zombie ninjas.

He'd gone head-to-head with his own cousin, Mai, who was more skilled in martial arts than anyone else in Japan.

But one thing truly scared him, and that was meeting Debbie Williams again.

Tom had been keeping out of Debbie's way for more than a month, ever since she'd asked him out to that party and he'd stood her up. It was the summer holidays, so he hadn't had to worry about sitting near Debbie in class or seeing her in lunch at school. However, she didn't live very far from where Tom did. He knew their paths were going to cross, sooner or later. And he wasn't looking forward to that at all.

In the end they met on a baking hot day in August. Tom had gone down to Camden Market to pick up some cheap games for his console. There was a stall at the market that sold them second-hand. Jaz, the stall owner, sometimes had beta-test versions of brand new games as well. It was against the law, but it was a good way of getting hold of the latest platform games and shoot-'em-ups long before they went on sale in the proper shops.

"*Grand Theft Auto: Paris,*" Jaz said in a low voice. He showed Tom a plain DVD-RW with the game title written on it in marker pen. "It's down for a Christmas release, although I've heard they might push it back to spring next year. It's really good. But they're still working on it so there are still some bugs in the software. The background doesn't always map the way it should. But that doesn't affect the game play, which is pretty awesome."

"How much?" Tom asked.

"For you, Tom, seeing as you're a regular – thirty."

"Thirty quid!" Tom was shocked.

"This is prime stuff, mate," said Jaz. "I've sold two dozen copies this week already. Everyone wants it."

"But I can buy it for just a tenner more if I wait till Christmas."

"If you wait till Christmas," Jaz said. He grinned, and there was a flash of metal from the three studs in his lip. "Question is, can you hang on that long?"

Tom frowned.

"After all," Jaz went on, "the world could end tomorrow. And then how would you feel? Pretty foolish, I'd bet. You'd be kicking yourself. You'd be saying, 'I wish I'd had a chance to play *GTA: Paris*, and now I never will!'"

"I don't think that's what I'd be saying if the world had just ended," Tom pointed out. "I think I'd be worrying about other things. That's if I was even alive."

"Hey." Jaz gave a shrug and dropped the disc into a box at his feet. "It's up to you. Thirty's my final offer."

Tom would have walked away. But it was Sharif's birthday soon, and Sharif was a total *Grand Theft Auto* nut. He'd been going on and on about the new one ever since he'd read online that it was coming out. Sharif would love to have a copy, dodgy knock-off or not.

"Twenty," Tom said.

Jaz raised his eyebrows. Both of them were pierced, like his lip. "Ah, so you are interested! And you'd like to haggle. OK, twenty-seven."

"Twenty-three pounds," Tom said in a firm voice.

"Twenty-five," said Jaz. "My final, final offer. Take it or leave it."

Tom gave a deep sigh. "All right."

"That's my man!" Jaz took Tom's money and handed him the disc in a brown paper bag. "It's always best to have something now, if you want it. Why wait? Life's short, and who knows when it's going to be over? Snatch at the moment. Live for today!"

These were truer words than Jaz knew. At least, for Tom they were. It wouldn't be long before he was fighting his next duel with the Five Lords of Pain. His fourth. This time, he was going to take on the Lord of the Typhoon. As Tom understood it, the Lord of the Typhoon was perhaps the most deadly of the five arch-demons. The only one of them who might be harder to beat was the Lord of Fire. Tom would have to face him if he won his duel with the Lord of the Typhoon.

Live for today? Tom didn't really have much of a choice.

"Tom?"

Tom had been wandering head down through the market, lost in thought. He looked up at the sound of his name.

It was Debbie Williams who'd spoken to him. Debbie was with two other girls. One was Natalie Bennett, who'd given the party Tom didn't go to. The other was someone Tom didn't know. Between the three of them they were holding at least twenty carrier bags. A massive girly clothes-shopping spree.

"Oh, er, Debbie," said Tom. "Hi." All at once he was feeling about three feet tall. His heart was thudding in his ears. He wished he could be somewhere else, anywhere, so long as it wasn't here.

Natalie was frowning at him. Debbie was looking at him as if he was a bit of a mystery to her. There was a hint of sadness in her eyes, too.

"You got something nice, then?" she said.

"Huh?"

"That." Debbie pointed at Tom's paper bag. "Something nice?"

So they were to have a polite chat. That was how Debbie wanted to play it, did she?

"Um, yeah," Tom said. "It's a present. For my friend Sharif. You know him. From school. Sharif Khan. Him with the bushy eyebrows. Good at science."

"I know who Sharif is," Debbie said. "Everyone does. He's the one who got attacked.

Knifed in the street outside his house. Poor thing. The police still haven't found who did it, have they?"

"And they never will," Tom said, without thinking.

The Shinobi Ghost who'd stabbed Sharif had vanished right after the attack. Tom's martial arts teacher Dragon had explained that a Shinobi Ghost was a dead person brought to life to do a job and then killed off again as soon as he'd finished his task. He had been dead once, and simply became dead again. His ninja clothes and weapons vanished by magic. All that was left was a naked body lying out in the open somewhere.

Dragon said the police would have found a man's body somewhere in London, a day or so after the attack on Sharif. They would most likely have been able to identify it and work out that it was the same dead body that had been reported missing from a hospital a few days earlier. They would have thought that the body had been stolen as some sort of sick prank, maybe. They'd never suspect that someone 6,000 miles away in Japan had cast a spell that gave new life to the body, armed it with ninja skills, and made it stand up and sneak out of the hospital.

What the police would also never suspect was that this mystery was linked to the mystery of who hurt Sharif. Why would they? There was nothing to connect the two cases, nothing to show that the naked body that had been dead for days had somehow been able to stick a dagger into Sharif more than twenty times. The police didn't deal in magic. They didn't believe that anyone had the power to turn a lifeless corpse into a ninja assassin. Therefore the police would never be able to find Sharif's attacker and bring him to justice.

Tom knew he shouldn't have said "And they never will" to Debbie. The moment the words left his lips, he wished he could take them back and pretend he'd never spoken them.

"How do you know that?" Debbie said. "You sound pretty sure."

"I meant … It came out the wrong way … All I was saying was …" Tom stammered.

"He's your friend," Debbie said. "Don't you want the cops to catch whoever hurt him?"

"Of course I do. Of course. It's just … I mean, the police haven't had much luck so far. You would have thought they'd have nabbed someone by now if they were going to. So it's, you know, not looking very good, that's all. That's what I was trying to say."

Tom couldn't decide if he was making things better or worse. One thing was for sure: he was jabbering away like an idiot.

"But I hope they do catch him," he went on, trying to sound as serious as he could. "I hope they get the guy and leave him to rot somewhere."

Which was, Tom thought, what had most likely happened already. In a sense.

Debbie gave him a funny look. "You're not like most other boys, are you, Tom?"

"Yeah," muttered Natalie. "Most other boys are *normal*."

The third girl giggled.

Tom felt his face going red. "I'm really sorry about the party, Debbie," he said.

"What party?" Debbie replied, her voice false and cool.

"You know, Natalie's party. The one I didn't turn up at."

"Oh, *that* party. I'd forgotten all about that. You didn't turn up? I don't remember that. Do you remember, Nats?"

Natalie shook her head. "Not me, Debs. Uh-uh. I didn't even know he was ever invited."

Now Tom felt about two feet tall, and getting smaller with every second. And he knew that was how Debbie wanted him to feel.

"Yeah, uh, something came up at the last moment," he said. "Something I couldn't get out of."

Brilliant excuse, he thought. *Just brilliant. Well done, Tom.*

"It's all right," Debbie said. "You were fixed up to go somewhere else. That's fine. I understand."

"But maybe we could, you know, meet up another time?"

Natalie scowled. "Yeah, right," she said out of the side of her mouth. "Good luck with that."

Tom took no notice of her. Debbie took no notice of her either – which made Tom think that not all hope was lost. Debbie might, just might, be thinking about forgiving him and giving him a second chance.

"I don't know," she said. "I've got a lot on. Why don't you let me have your phone number? We'll see how it goes."

Tom took out his phone, ready to swap with Debbie. But Debbie just gave him her phone and told him to tap his number into the memory. She didn't take Tom's phone.

Tom handed her phone back when he had finished inputting the number. Now, Debbie had his number but he didn't have hers. Everything was up to her. Debbie would decide if they were going to get in touch, not Tom.

"See you around," Debbie said, and she moved off. Natalie and the other girl followed her.

Before they were out of earshot, Tom heard Natalie hiss, "What on Earth do you see in him, Debs? He's such a loser."

"I don't know," Debbie replied. "He may be a loser, but he's a cute loser."

It wasn't much of a compliment. But coming from Debbie Williams, it made Tom's whole day.

Chapter 2
Email From Mai

At home, Tom grabbed some corn chips and a bottle of Lucozade and switched on his computer. He was off to train with Dragon in an hour's time. He thought he would check his email and do a little surfing on the internet first.

There was a message from his cousin Mai in his inbox. Tom shoved a fistful of corn chips into his mouth and clicked Read.

The email began:

Dear True Warrior

Mai had chosen the nickname for Tom based on something the Lord of Tears had said. Tom, in turn, always began his emails to Mai "Dear Chop-Socky Chick", which she liked.

Tom was pleased that he and his cousin had become friends. They'd got off to a bad start. Since then, however, they had been in contact by email and become quite close. They swapped tips on fighting styles. They discussed what was different about England and Japan and what was the same. They talked about their favourite martial arts movies. (Tom's number one choice was a tie between *Ong-Bak* and *Kung Fu Hustle*, while Mai preferred *Enter the Dragon*, "the old-school Bruce Lee classic", as she put it.)

They also talked about the Yamada family. They chatted about what it was like to be a member of the clan, what it meant to be part of all that Contest history. This was something

Tom couldn't talk about with anyone else, except his mother, and she was no great fan of the Yamadas. The only Yamada she was willing to talk about was her dead husband, Kenji. She had loved Tom's father like mad, and still missed him like mad.

Mai sent Tom little written sketches of her relatives in Japan – her parents, her older brother and two younger sisters, her other cousins, and of course his great-aunt Akiko, that spidery-eyed old witch. Tom learned all about their good and bad points, the kind things they did and the stupid things as well. Mai's emails often made him laugh out loud. Thanks to her, he'd begun to feel connected with that side of his family in a way he never had before. He felt his Japanese roots more and more strongly. He felt more of a Yamada.

Today, Mai's email was different. It wasn't chatty or witty. Tom felt his stomach start to knot as he read the email.

I've just had a visit from my grandmother. She was in a very odd mood. I've never seen Akiko-san so worried and so serious. She had a warning for you, which she has asked me to pass on. She said it was urgent that you be told this.

It's about your trainer, Dragon.

My grandmother said she has been asking about him among her contacts in the martial arts world. She has also been using magic to find out what she can about him. She consulted the tarot cards. She did a number-reading of Dragon's name in *kanji*. She cast her fortune-telling stones and read their message.

Akiko-san wants you to know that Dragon is not all that he seems. She would like you to ask yourself some questions about him. When did you first meet him? How did you meet him? Why did you agree to let him train you?

Akiko-san says consider the answers with care. They might tell you something you didn't see before.

Tom, I don't know what my grandmother means by any of this. I don't know why she's giving you all these hints. If she has found out something about Dragon, something important which you ought to know, then why doesn't she just tell you?

I'm aware that there is no great love between you and Akiko-san.

But I think you should listen to what she is saying.

Tom sat back in his chair, frowning.

What was this? What game was Great-aunt Akiko playing here?

Great-aunt Akiko didn't like Dragon. Tom remembered how rude Dragon had been to her when they'd met in the Black Forest. Dragon had called her "an evil little toad" and had been angry with her for trying to replace Tom with Mai as the Contest champion. Great-aunt

Akiko had told Dragon that she would get her own back on him for the way he had insulted her. Dragon hadn't seemed too bothered by this, even though Great-aunt Akiko was a bad enemy to have, in Tom's view.

Now Great-aunt Akiko wanted Tom to ask himself questions about his *sensei*.

Tom had a pretty good idea what she was trying to do. She was messing with his head. She was trying to make him suspect Dragon, to mistrust him.

But why? Did she want Tom to stop training with Dragon? Was her plan to drive a wedge between the two of them? If so, that was crazy. Great-aunt Akiko knew how important the Contest was. In spite of everything else, she was a Yamada through and through. She wouldn't dare put the outcome of the Contest at risk. She knew what was at stake. She knew Tom needed to go on getting the best training possible.

So what did she hope to gain by getting Mai to pass on this "warning" of hers about Dragon?

Tom was still puzzling it over as he got on the bus to go to Dragon's *dojo*.

Chapter 3
The Need for Pain

Dragon walked in a circle round Tom.

"Right hand a little higher," he said. "Make the movements flow. No breaks between them. Glide from one to the next, like waves. The *sai* must be a part of your own body. They are your hands. Draw back with the left one. Now thrust! That's it. Now, ice-pick grip. Turn both *sai* back along your arm. Index finger along handle. There. Your balance is OK, Tom, but try to keep your knees looser. Your legs must be like springs. Whatever happens down below, your upper body should stay stable. So if, for example, you get hit like *this* ..."

Dragon kicked Tom's shin. He didn't do it hard, but just enough for Tom to feel it.

"... you still keep control of your weapons," Dragon finished.

Tom's leg had wobbled when Dragon kicked him, but the two *sai* went on smoothly through the air.

"Not bad," Dragon said, still walking in a circle. "Now, block."

Tom crossed the *sai* in front of him, so that their blades locked together in an X. As he did so, Dragon kicked him again, this time in the back of the knee.

The kick was hard. And it hurt.

Still, Tom was just able to hold his balance.

"And 'bumper' the *sai*," Dragon ordered.

Tom swung both of the fork-like daggers up and inward, so that he was holding each of them by its central prong. The U-shaped guards covered his hands.

Dragon swung his foot right at Tom's kneecap.

Pain burst up Tom's leg. He couldn't stay standing any more. The whole leg went numb. He sank to the floor, grunting in agony.

He looked up at Dragon, with his eyes watering. "What did you go and do that for?" he demanded.

"To see what it would take to break your focus," Dragon replied. "And it turns out the answer is: not much."

"That bloody hurt," Tom said, rubbing his knee. "There was no call for that."

"No call?" said Dragon. His orange-brown eyes went wide. Tom knew Dragon was about to blow his top. "*No call?* Listen to yourself.

26

Did you hear what you just said? Do you think your training should be soft? Is that it? Do you think I should go easy on you?"

"No," said Tom. "I just – "

"Maybe I should only have given you a little tap," Dragon went on. "Maybe we should be playing around with feather dusters, not real weapons. Would you prefer that? And why don't I put a nice thick rug down on the floor as well, and put on some lovely music in the background? And how about you wear a pink ballet skirt while we're about it?"

"*Sensei*, all I was saying – "

Dragon shouted over his protests. "Training has nothing to do with being fair or kind, Tom," he yelled. "It has nothing to do with me showing you mercy or being gentle. It can't have. And you know why? Because your enemies don't show mercy. They aren't gentle. You need to be tough to fight them. My job is to make you tough. And that means pain, from

27

time to time. They're called the Lords of Pain, after all. Not the Lords of Love, or Pity, or Kindness. The clue's in the name. Now get up."

Tom did manage to stand up, but it was hard.

"Lift those *sai*."

Tom raised the daggers.

"Go on with your *kata* exercises."

Tom began moving the *sai* again, running through the set patterns he had been shown. His knee throbbed. He gritted his teeth against the pain.

Dragon paced to the far end of the room, then came back.

"The Lord of the Typhoon is nothing like the three Lords of Pain you've already met, Tom," he said. He was a bit more calm now. "The Lord of the Typhoon is a force of nature,

like the storm he is named after. You can't
work out where he will go next. He is pure
power and fury. Going up against him is like
going up against a hurricane. He will not give
you a moment's rest. He will hammer at you
from the beginning of the duel right to the
very end."

"Yes, *sensei*."

"And there is one other thing you should
know about him," Dragon said. "The Lord of
the Typhoon was the last Lord of Pain your
father had to fight. He gave your father the
wounds that he died of in the end."

Tom's blood ran cold. "You mean ...?"

"The Lord of the Typhoon killed your
father, Tom," said Dragon. "Now you
understand what a danger he is? And why I
must be harsh with you? Why there can be no
slacking here?"

Tom gave a grim nod.

29

The *sai* trembled in his hands. He stopped doing his *kata* and jabbed the *sai* forwards in a one-two stab. Then he did it again. Then again. As if the Lord of the Typhoon was standing right in front of him, and Tom was plunging the daggers into the arch-demon's chest, over and over again.

Dragon's mouth turned up at the corners – a sort of smile.

Chapter 4

How Dragon Came Into Tom's Life

Tom's training sessions got even more harsh over the next few days. He was used to leaving the *dojo* with a couple of fresh bruises from time to time. Now, however, he was coming home black and blue every time.

Dragon wasn't sparing him. Dragon wasn't holding back. Dragon was being harder on him than he'd ever been.

It was for Tom's own good, or so Dragon said. Dragon claimed he was getting Tom into

shape for his duel with the Lord of the
Typhoon.

But since when did "getting him into shape"
mean knocking him to bits?

What was worse, Tom couldn't shake off
the feeling that Dragon was enjoying it.
Dragon was getting a kick out of kicking him.
He was punch-drunk from punching him.
Every time Tom cried out in pain, Dragon
seemed to find it funny. The golden flecks in
those orange-brown eyes of his glinted
brighter than ever.

Or did I imagine that? thought Tom.

He wasn't sure. He was still disturbed by
the email from Mai. Great-aunt Akiko clearly
wanted him not to trust Dragon. So Tom was
doing his best to trust Dragon even more than
ever, in order to spite Great-aunt Akiko. But
he couldn't quite do it. Great-aunt Akiko's
warning had wormed its way deep into his
brain. He couldn't stop thinking about it.

"Mum," Tom said one evening.

Jane Yamada looked up from her Sudoku puzzle. She was watching an old episode of *CSI* on their new flatscreen TV at the same time. And drinking wine. She was a true multi-tasker, Tom's mother.

"Yes, Tom?"

"Dragon."

"What about him?"

"I've been thinking ..." Tom began.

"Careful," said his mother. "You could hurt yourself doing that."

"Oh, ha ha," said Tom. "I've been thinking," he carried on, "where does Dragon come from?"

"From north London."

"You know what I mean. Where from before that? He wasn't born here. What country does he belong to?"

"I've no idea. China? India? Malaysia? Looking at him, it's hard to tell. It could be he's a mix of several races. He's not from Japan, that much I do know. He doesn't speak the language. I tried. I said '*ohayo*' to him one morning. He looked at me as if I'd just sneezed. Anyway, his accent when he speaks English is not at all Japanese."

"But that's my point," Tom said. "What accent is it? It's sort of Asian. Far Eastern for sure. But where in the Far East? I've never heard an accent like it, and I've watched a hell of a lot of Far Eastern films."

"Accents can change. Maybe Dragon's been living in England so long, he's picked up some of our ways of saying words. His accent has got some London-talk mixed up in it, and who knows what else. That's why it doesn't sound like any accent you know."

Tom's mother rubbed out a number she'd written in her Sudoku grid and wrote in another.

"Why not simply ask him where's from?" she went on. "I'm sure he'd be happy to tell you."

"I suppose I could," said Tom. "But Dragon's always been so unwilling to talk about himself. I don't even know his real name. Do you?"

"Nope," said his mother.

"But don't you write him a cheque every month, for my training fees?"

"I make it out to the Dragon Martial Arts Academy, not to Dragon himself."

"And he sort of wandered into our lives, didn't he?" Tom said. "It was when you were beginning to look for someone to train me for the Contest …"

"... and I was going through the small ads in the back of the local paper one day," said his mother, "and there it was. Dragon's ad. It offered first class lessons 'in all the main Eastern martial arts', if I remember right."

"No, that wasn't quite it, was it?" said Tom.

"I think it was, Tom."

"No, Mum, remember? You came across that ad *after* I'd already been training with Dragon for two months."

Jane Yamada sucked the end of her pencil. "You know, you're right. I forgot that. We met him in the park, didn't we?"

Tom nodded. "Up on Hampstead Heath. We passed by him. He was standing out on the grass, doing some *kata*. He nodded at us as we walked past along the path. Then later I was in the playground, mucking about on the climbing frame, and Dragon came over to talk to you."

"That's it. Yes," said his mother. "You do have a good memory, Tom. Unlike me."

"It's all right, Mum. It's not your fault. You're old. Your brain cells are dying."

"They are," said his mother, with a sigh. She frowned down at her Sudoku. "That, or the people who set these puzzles are making them harder every day."

"Can you remember what Dragon said to you?"

"In the playground? Well, it was years ago, and my poor dying brain cells can't remember all the detail. But he did say something about how good your balance was. He said he'd been watching you with delight because you moved with such grace. I have to say my first thought then was, *What's going on in this man's twisted mind? What does he want with my Tom?* I was all set to thump him and yell for the police. But Dragon went on about your being so co-ordinated. Your reflexes were so good. He said he'd never seen a child your age with such inborn athletic skills. And he asked me if you'd ever had martial arts training, or if I'd ever thought about getting you some. And I remember thinking, *That's funny, because it's about time Tom started training for the Contest.* And I said something along those lines to Dragon, only I didn't mention the Contest of course. And Dragon said, 'Well then, madam, may I humbly offer my services as your son's trainer. I believe he would make a wonderful pupil.' And he gave me his card, and said I'd find his rates very fair. And that was that, really. He seemed like someone you could trust. And I went along to your first few training sessions with you, just to make sure everything was on the up and up, and I was impressed by him.

"Dragon seemed as if he could provide you with everything you would need for the Contest. I don't know that much about martial arts, but I know some, thanks to your father.

And Dragon was clearly very skilled, and you seemed to get on with him. So it all just sort of ... fell into place, didn't it? We met the right person at the right time. As if it was meant to be."

"Hmm," said Tom.

"What do you mean, 'hmm'?" said his mother. "Don't you think it was your lucky day, meeting Dragon like that? You've done all right by him. Better than all right, in fact. Three Lords of Pain down, two to go. I'd say things have worked out rather well. More than well, given that you're half the age a Contest champion should be."

"Yeah," said Tom, "I know. But something's bothering me. Looking back, don't you feel it was all a bit neat? Dragon being there on the Heath that day. Him spotting me. The whole thing."

"Neat? But that's not always a bad thing."

"But more than that. Like … like it was something Dragon planned. Something he made happen."

"How could he have made it happen, Tom?" said his mother. "He didn't know you and I were going to be there that day, at that time."

"He could have staked out the playground before then," Tom said. "He could have been watching us for several days. We always used the same route to get to the playground, didn't we? We always walked along that same path, right by the spot where we saw him practising his *kata*. And we always did it at about the same time each day. Three-thirty, just after school had finished. You were working flexi-time then, so you could always come and pick me up from school. All Dragon would have had to do was spy on us from a distance till he was sure he'd got our routine worked out. Then it was just a case of him waiting at the right place at the right time, and bingo. He planned to meet us, but made it look as if it was by chance."

"Tom!" His mother looked amazed. "What's up with you? You make it sound as if it was all some sneaky plot to trap you. As if Dragon knew who you were and wanted to get his hands on you."

"Well, isn't it just possible?"

"Only if you're paranoid. Why would Dragon bother to plan it like that? What was in it for him?"

"Me," said Tom. "Getting me as his pupil."

"Don't be such a big-head."

"I'm not. It must be a big thing for any martial arts trainer, having the Contest champion as his pupil. It'd be something to brag about."

"It would," said his mother, "if the Contest weren't a secret. Dragon had never heard of

41

the Contest when he started training you. I left it at least a year before telling him about it. He didn't even believe me to begin with. He asked around among his contacts in the martial arts world to see if anyone else knew about it. All he got back was very hazy and unclear information. Most people told him it was just a myth, a story. It was ages before he believed that the Contest was real. So that couldn't have been why he offered to train you. You can't brag if no one else has a clue what you're bragging about."

"I suppose so," said Tom with a slight nod. He was thinking.

"What's started this?" said his mother. "Why are you being so weird and hostile about Dragon all of a sudden?"

Tom wanted to tell her. He wanted to tell her about Great-aunt Akiko's message, and also about that time in the hotel in Tokyo, when he'd thought he'd seen Dragon's eyes fill up with a fiery light. It had only been for a moment. Now he wanted to say that he wasn't sure any more that Dragon wished him well. He wanted to say that he was even starting to be a little bit afraid of Dragon.

But in the end all he said was, "It's nothing, Mum. Me being silly, that's all. I'm pretty tired. I expect that's it." He faked a yawn. "I might just go to bed. That OK with you?"

Jane Yamada poured herself another glass of wine.

"You do that, Tom," she said. "See you in the morning."

Tom put on his pyjamas and lay in bed, staring up into the darkness.

Was he being paranoid?

Common sense said he was.

The pain of his many bruises said different.

Chapter 5

Can Save the World but Can't Drink

Tom went to the bank vault with his mother. Together, they opened the black wooden box and studied the five Element Gems inside.

Three of the gems pulsed with a feeble light. These were the three that had been removed from the hearts of the Lord of the Mountain, the Lord of the Void and the Lord of Tears. A fourth gem, which was bright red, glowed strongly. This was the Lord of Fire's.

The fifth gem belonged to the Lord of the Typhoon. It was sea green in colour, and it had begun to fade out. It looked like a ghost beside the other four. You could see all the way through it.

"Not long, then," said Tom's mother.

"Wonder where I'll be going this time," Tom said. "Hope it's not another long-distance flight, like to Australia. I wouldn't mind it being somewhere nice and tropical. Maybe a Caribbean island. I could lie on a beach, soak up some sun, drink a few rum punches ..."

"Dream on," said his mother. "No rum punches for you till the law says you're old enough."

Tom gave a hollow laugh. "Yeah. I'm old enough to save the world, but not old enough to drink alcohol. What's up with that?"

His mother laughed too. "Tell you what. I promise, when the Contest is over, we'll go to the Caribbean. I'll take a month off work. Sharif can come too. We deserve it, all of us. It'll be our reward."

"Cool! And maybe I can have just one rum punch? To see if I like it?"

His mother gave him a playful cuff round the ear. "Don't push it, mister."

It was Sharif's birthday the next day. He didn't have a big party. He'd left hospital only a week earlier, and the doctors had advised that he shouldn't do anything too exciting or active for a while. So it was just the Khan family at the party, and Tom.

Sharif had five sisters, two older, three younger. All of them fussed over him, making sure he was comfortable in his chair and fetching extra cushions for him, even if he didn't want them. Mrs Khan had laid on plenty of food and baked a huge chocolate cake. When the cake was carried in Mr Khan made a short speech about Sharif, saying how glad he was to have his son back home. He thanked Allah for sparing Sharif's life and ...

The speech would have lasted longer but Mr Khan was too choked with emotion to carry on. He wiped his eyes and told Sharif to blow out the candles. Sharif did, and everyone ate the cake. Tom had two slices, and then a third, but only because Mrs Khan insisted.

Then Tom and Sharif played the new *Grand Theft Auto* game together. Sharif said it was the coolest present anyone had ever given him. The two of them spent a happy hour crashing cars and mowing down people on the pavement and generally making the streets of Paris as unsafe as possible.

At last Tom had to go home. Sharif walked him to the front door. Tom was sad to see the way Sharif moved. He was stiff and slow, like an old man, because of his injuries. Every step seemed painful.

Tom knew he himself wasn't to blame for what had happened to Sharif. But he also knew that Sharif would never have been hurt if he hadn't been Tom's friend. It made Tom hate Great-aunt Akiko even more.

Two days after that, the challenge came.

Tom heard a loud *whurrumph* from the flat's kitchen, like an electric motor with a bad cough. This was followed by an enormous *crash*.

The extractor fan above the cooker had exploded. The whole unit had come loose from its fittings and smashed onto the gas hob below.

Tom's mother gave a shrug when she saw the damage.

"Could have been worse," she said. "It's not as if we use the cooker much. Thank God the microwave's still in one piece."

Tom fished a scroll out from the broken extractor fan. He undid the sea-green ribbon that was tied round the scroll. Then he unrolled the piece of parchment and pretended to read the *kanji* symbols written on it.

"'The Lord of the Typhoon would like to offer his regrets. He's a yellow-bellied coward and he knows that Tom Yamada is going to beat him nine ways to Sunday, so he's calling off the duel.'"

"If only," said his mother. "Give me that."

She scanned the scroll quickly.

"Well, it's not too bad," she said. "You're off to Greece, Tom. One of the Greek islands. The weather should be nice there this time of year."

"No, it won't," said Tom. "You forget. There's always rubbish weather at the site of a duel."

"True," his mother admitted. "But at least it's only three hours on the plane."

Chapter 6
The Burning Island

More like four hours on the plane. Then a taxi ride from the airport to Athens harbour. And then a long trip on a tourist boat, out across the Mediterranean Sea.

The sun shone in a clear sky. There was a light breeze, which took the edge off the fierce heat. The sea was a smooth carpet of blue. There was no sign of the rubbish weather Tom had been expecting.

But then Theo, the captain of the boat, told them about the island they were going to. He said it had been hit by a terrible electrical storm two days ago.

"Is very, very bad storm," said Theo. "So bad, no one can remember one like it. Much lightning. Comes down – *zap*! Sets the forest alight. Some fires still burning now, but most under control. Half of island is big mess. All black and smoking. But other half of island OK. Safe. The main town safe. And the beaches. You'll be OK. Have nice holiday."

The island came into view on the horizon. It looked normal enough, till the boat got closer. Then Tom could see a dark haze in the air, hovering over the island like an enormous shadow, like some kind of angel of death. He could also smell the burning – a faint whiff of smoke, carried on the breeze.

"No prize for guessing where we'll be heading tomorrow," he muttered to Dragon.

Dragon said nothing. His gaze was fixed on the horizon. Tom could see that the golden flecks in Dragon's eyes were dancing. Dancing for joy.

But maybe they were just reflecting the sunlight that dazzled on the sea's surface.

The island's main town was a port. There was a harbour and hundreds of white houses that climbed the slope of the island in a jumble. There were a dozen newly built hotels spread out along the shoreline. They looked like a line of huge white sugar cubes. All of them looked out over a long, sandy beach.

Tom, his mother and Dragon checked into one of these hotels, the Hotel Herakles. Herakles was another name for Hercules, the hero of Ancient Greek myth. Tom took this as a good omen. Hercules, after all, had faced a series of hard tasks, called the Twelve Labours, which were his punishment for killing his own wife and children in a fit of madness. He'd carried out all twelve with great success, and as a reward the gods had made him immortal, so, like themselves, he would never die.

There were pictures painted on the walls of the hotel lobby. They showed Hercules killing a lion, fighting with a bull, and getting on with all the other tasks he had been set. Tom went round studying them all. He himself had only five "labours" to complete, and there was no promise that he would live forever if he got through them all. But still the pictures cheered him up. Hercules had battled against tremendous odds, and won. So would Tom.

For dinner, Tom, his mother and Dragon ate tomatoes stuffed with rice, vine leaves stuffed with rice, and roast chicken. Tom half-expected the chicken to be stuffed with rice as well, but it wasn't. His mother tried some of the local wine, called retsina. She said it tasted like bleach, but she still managed to drink most of the bottle.

Dragon seemed very distant during the meal. Their table was on a terrace next to the beach. Dragon kept looking out to sea, at the sunset. He spoke only when Tom or Tom's mother said something directly to him. Otherwise he stared at the sun as it went down. Its blazing light seemed to set the waves on fire.

Night came. Insects chirped outside the window to Tom's room. There seemed to be millions of them, and the sound they made was far too loud. Tom hardly slept at all.

Next morning, Tom's mother drove them to the other side of the island in a rented car.

Tom was about to meet the Lord of the Typhoon.

The demon who'd killed his father.

Payback time.

Chapter 7
"Who Are You?"

The landscape was black and charred. Bushes were just piles of ash. Trees were bare and shrivelled, as if drawn in pencil against a pale sky. Here and there the ground was still alight, glowing orange. Some houses were smoking ruins, hollow and gutted. Others had got away with just a few scorch marks.

Tom's mother knew where they had to go. There was a holy place up on a clifftop. Long ago, a temple with a shrine had stood there. People used to travel to the shrine to consult a priestess who could tell the future. You could ask the priestess questions, in return for gifts of food and wine. She spoke with the gods and passed back the answers they gave, telling you when to plant crops, who you should marry, whether the fishing would be good this year, and so on.

Now nothing was left of the shrine except a few piles of broken stones and a couple of the pillars which had held up its roof. The shrine was in the middle of a grove of sacred olive trees. Plenty of olive trees still grew on the spot – or at any rate did before the fire.

Not all of the roads on the island were in use. Some were blocked off by signs that warned *Fire* and *Danger*, in both Greek and English. Nevertheless Tom's mother was able to get the car quite close to the site of the shrine. She parked by the roadside. Tom and Dragon continued on foot, trudging up a steep hill over black earth and brittle grass.

The silence was huge. And terrible.

Dragon halted near the top of the hill, not far from the site of the clifftop shrine. Tom could hear the waves crashing against the base of the nearby cliff. Dragon set down his sports bag full of weapons. Tom changed into his combat *gi*. He showed up very clearly in his white uniform, against all the blackness around him. And he knew it.

Dragon loaded Tom up with *sai*, *katana*, *shuriken*, *chigiriki*, and *nunchaku*.

"Whoa," said Tom, feeling how heavy the weapons felt hanging off him. "Not taking any chances, are we?"

"No," said Dragon, his voice grave. "We are not. Truly, this is the most dangerous fight you've ever taken part in, Tom. You must give it all you've got. Show the Lord of the Typhoon no mercy. Bring out every last bit of courage and *kiai* in your body. Destroy him, and bring me back that Element Gem."

"You mean bring back that Element Gem," Tom said. "Not bring you back."

"That's what I said," said Dragon.

"No, you didn't."

"Well, it's what I meant."

Tom stared at his *sensei*. The time had come. He couldn't wait any longer to ask the question that had been bugging him for days.

"Who are you, Dragon?"

Dragon seemed taken aback. "What kind of question is that?" he said, blinking. "I'm your *sensei*. I'm your master. You know this."

"But who *are* you?" Tom insisted. "I've known you for seven years, but I feel I hardly know you at all."

"I'm the person who's trained you to the very highest level. I'm the person who's got you ready for the Contest. That's what you know about me, Tom. And that should be all you need to know."

"But it isn't," said Tom. "It isn't all I need to know. Not any more."

"Go," Dragon said. He flapped his hand, urging Tom to start walking. "It's time for the duel. You'll be late."

Tom set off up towards the shrine. Then he stopped and turned.

"This little chat of ours isn't over, Dragon," he said.

"I look forward to carrying on with it," Dragon replied. "When you've come back with that gem."

Chapter 8
The Lord of the Typhoon

Tom entered the arena, through its gateway of shimmering mist. He'd become used to the balloon-like feeling in the pit of his stomach, that sense of going up in a lift fast, as he crossed between worlds. He was hardly aware of it.

He had time to notice the audience of demons gathered outside the arena. There seemed to be more of them, compared with the last three duels.

He also had time to notice that the arena went right up to the very edge of the cliff. The sea beyond was scarlet in colour, and was boiling like soup in a hot pan. Tom could smell it, and it didn't smell of salt water like an ordinary sea. It smelled of rotten eggs. Of sulphur.

Then there was a sound like a huge, rushing wind. Something hit Tom head-on, hard. He was lifted off his feet, carried through the air, and slammed back down onto the ground.

He dragged himself back up again, only to be hit once more, from behind this time. He was swept along, with his feet bumping and scraping over stones. He was thrown against a large rock. Some gut instinct made Tom go limp, so as to allow his body to take the shock better. Still, it hurt as he whammed into the rock. It hurt like hell.

A hand grabbed Tom by the collar before he could recover his senses. He was yanked up off the ground. He felt himself being spun round and round. Then the hand let go, and Tom flew towards the cliff edge. He landed just inches from it. He saw the scarlet sea out of the corner of his eye. It lay 100 metres or more below. Waves crashed against the cliff, sending up a hissing, steaming spray. Tom sprang away from the edge, scrambling towards the centre of the arena.

Battered, bruised, tossed about ... and he hadn't even had seen his opponent yet. Let alone managed to draw a weapon.

Tom heard the rushing-wind sound again. It was coming from his left. He leapt to his right, throwing himself flat on the ground. Something whooshed over him. He saw green skin and a pair of leathery, bat-like wings. He pounced upright, sliding his *katana* from its sheath at the same time.

The Lord of the Typhoon turned in mid-air and swooped at Tom. He was like some ugly bird of prey. He came down with wings flat and arms outstretched. His fingers ended in claw-like talons. His ears were large and pointed, and his mouth was filled with fangs. There was a fin on top of his head, like a lizard's crest. His eyes were spaced far apart and stuck out. They glowed red, which Tom had come to know was the mark of a Lord of Pain.

It took Tom just an instant to make sense of all he had seen. An instant was all he got. That was how long it took the Lord of the Typhoon to dive at him. Tom couldn't believe how fast the arch-demon could fly. Next to him, the Lord of Tears seemed a slowcoach.

Tom thrust out with his *katana*. It was a moment of despair. He hoped the sword would find its target but he didn't expect it to.

And it didn't. The Lord of the Typhoon twisted around the blade and smashed right into Tom. Tom found himself being pushed backwards across the arena. He dug his heels in but it didn't make any difference. The Lord of the Typhoon pushed and pushed, with his wings beating strongly. He was driving Tom towards the cliff edge. He was going to shove him over.

Chapter 9
Nunchaku Attack

There was only one thing to do. Tom let the Lord of the Typhoon push him close to the cliff edge, almost all the way. Then, at the last possible moment, he let his legs collapse under him, so that he fell flat on his back.

The sudden shift in balance caught the Lord of the Typhoon by surprise. He lost his grip on Tom and went shooting onwards to the cliff edge. He shot over, vanishing out of sight.

Tom knew better than to think the Lord of the Typhoon was going to fall to his death. The arch-demon had wings, after all.

But it took the Lord of the Typhoon several seconds to open his wings, check his fall, come soaring upwards, and return to the arena.

Several seconds, in which Tom was able to put away his *katana*, pull out his *nunchaku*, and get a handful of *shuriken* ready.

When the Lord of the Typhoon came into view again, Tom let him have it. He flung the *shuriken* one after another at the arch-demon. Three of the throwing-stars thudded into the Lord of the Typhoon's chest, and he cried out in pain. He landed clumsily, and Tom ran at him, spinning the *nunchaku* above his head like a helicopter blades. He hit the Lord of the Typhoon everywhere – face, neck, belly, between the legs, all the soft and tender places. He used horizontal strikes, 90-degree strikes, diagonal strikes, with brief stop-moves in between. He didn't pause once. He gave it everything he had. The *nunchaku* whirled and whacked, whirled and whacked, over and over. The Lord of the Typhoon kept grunting and trying to block the blows. But Tom didn't stop. He couldn't stop. He wouldn't stop.

You killed my dad, he was thinking.

Tom had never known his father. To him, Kenji Yamada was a face in photographs and a person his mother often talked about. That was all. Tom didn't feel any love for the man. How could he? To love someone you had to have known them.

But a father was a father. Half of Tom had come from Kenji Yamada. He carried his father's looks, and his father's DNA, and he had some of his father's habits as well, according to his mother. The same way of tilting his head to the side when something puzzled him. The same way of tugging on his earlobe when he didn't like what was going on.

Tom's mother was fond of saying, "Ken would have been a wonderful dad. He would have known how to raise you and look after you, Tom. He would have done a better job of it than I ever could."

And that was what made Tom truly angry. That was why he pounded the Lord of the Typhoon without mercy, and why he wasn't going to waste the chance to hurt the arch-demon, now that he had one.

Because the Lord of the Typhoon had taken something from Tom. He'd taken the time Tom should have had with his father. He'd taken fifteen years during which Tom should have lived with a mum *and* a dad.

And, what was more, the Lord of the Typhoon had made Tom's mother a widow. Tom's mother had never got over the loss of her husband. She never would. His death had left a wound in her soul that wouldn't ever heal. She would carry her grief to the grave.

Tom's attack with the *nunchaku* went on for several minutes. The Lord of the Typhoon wasn't able to fight back. He tried to fly away, but Tom just grabbed him by one wing, held him down, and kept hitting him. He stopped using the *nunchaku* the way Dragon had taught him, the way he should have used it. He just bashed away with it, as if it was a kind of club.

It felt really good. Tom was grinning. The Lord of the Typhoon's yelps and howls were music to his ears.

In the end the Lord of the Typhoon sagged to his knees, groaning. Tom stepped back. His arm was tired and aching. The *nunchaku* dangled from his hand, dripping crimson. Blood trickled all over the Lord of the Typhoon, dark red against his green skin.

The Lord of the Typhoon's head was bowed. To Tom, he looked beaten.

Tom got ready to draw his *katana* and deliver the killing blow.

Then the Lord of the Typhoon's body started to shake and heave. A low, deep rumble filled the air.

Laughter.

The Lord of the Typhoon was laughing.

He raised his head. His smile was broad. Savage. Full of glee.

"Why did you stop, Yamada?" he said. "You should have kept going till I was nothing but pulp. That mistake will cost you."

He side-swiped Tom with one wing. The bony edge of the wing smacked Tom in the chest, hard as an iron bar. Tom felt something snap inside him.

The force of the blow bowled him over. Tom lay on his side. Every breath hurt. He seemed to have splinters of glass in his chest, digging into his lungs. A rib. A broken rib. Must be.

The Lord of the Typhoon rose up and stood over him, casting a shadow onto Tom's face.

"Unlike my fellow Lords of Pain, I am a creature of few words," he said. "The others like to talk. I like to *do*."

He raised one hand with its long talons. They glinted wickedly in the dark sunlight.

"Your father screamed when I cut him," the Lord of the Typhoon said. "I remember it well. A high-pitched sound. Like a baby's cry. I wonder if you'll do the same."

He slashed down at Tom's face.

Chapter 10
Brutal and Ugly

Tom tried to escape the blow.

He very nearly did.

The Lord of the Typhoon's talons raked his cheek. They would have had one of Tom's eyes out, if Tom had moved any more slowly.

Still, the pain was awful. It was impossible to describe. Tom felt as if half his face had been ripped away. Blood slooshed down his jaw and neck, hot and slick. The smell of it filled his nose. His own blood. A thick and sickly smell.

Tom did not scream.

He wanted to, but he refused to. Not after what the Lord of the Typhoon had said, mocking him about his father. Tom wouldn't let the arch-demon have the pleasure of hearing *him* scream too.

The Lord of the Typhoon raised his hand again. His talons were shining with Tom's blood.

Tom shut out the pain. He moved fast. His hand went to his belt. It grasped the hilt of one of the weapons there.

The Lord of the Typhoon's hand came down.

Tom's hand came up at the same time.

"Aaieee!!!"

The Lord of the Typhoon reeled away, holding out his hand. One of Tom's *sai* was sticking through the hand. The central prong of the *sai* had gone in through the palm and out the back.

Tom got weakly to his feet, drawing his other *sai*. He felt dizzy. The pain made him want to throw up.

The Lord of the Typhoon grabbed the hilt of the *sai* that had gone through his hand. He began tugging at it to work the *sai* free. He whimpered and cried out as he did so.

"Now who's the baby?" Tom said. Or at least tried to say. His mouth wouldn't work properly, thanks to the gash in his cheek. The words came out as "Ow ooz ver vayvee?"

Best save the jokes for later, Tom told himself.

He lurched forwards. The simple act of walking was agony. Every footstep jarred his broken rib. He could almost feel the two jagged ends of bone grinding against each other.

But he kept going.

The Lord of the Typhoon was still trying to pull the *sai* out of his hand.

He turned his head as Tom came staggering towards him.

Tom thrust out with his *sai* before the Lord of the Typhoon could move against him. Tom's aim was off. He'd been going for the arch-demon's chest. Instead, he got one of his wings. The *sai* cut clean through the skin of the wing. Tom slashed downwards with it. The skin split open. It wasn't nearly as tough as it looked. It tore like silk. Tom ripped open one whole section of the wing.

The Lord of the Typhoon let out a wail. He leapt into the air in order to get away from Tom. It was a simple reflex for him – to fly out of harm's way.

But one of his wings was useless now, a tattered, bleeding thing. He couldn't fly. He flapped his other wing but it couldn't create enough lift by itself. The Lord of the Typhoon came tumbling back to earth, landing in a heap.

Tom didn't stop to think. He was swaying. He was on his last legs. He couldn't let the fight drag on a moment longer.

He flipped the *sai* so that the central prong was pointing downwards. He bent down over the body of the Lord of the Typhoon. He stabbed him in the throat.

Then in the chest.

Then in the stomach.

And then he stabbed him some more.

And some more.

The *sai* went up and down, up and down. It got bloodier each time. Soon little lumps of skin and flesh were sticking to it.

Tom kept stabbing till long after his enemy was dead. At some point he knew he could stop stabbing. But it was some time later that he did.

He collapsed. He was crying with relief, and pain.

It hadn't been a pretty fight. It had been brutal and ugly. Martial arts skills had gone out of the window. So had style. Tom hadn't simply been battling the Lord of the Typhoon. He'd been battling for his life.

But he had won.

He'd won!

And he had avenged his father's death.

Tom knew that he shouldn't cheer. With his broken rib and torn face, it would hurt. A lot.

He cheered anyway.

Chapter 11
Carrying on the Little Chat

Tom tottered out of the arena, back into the burnt black landscape of the Greek island. He was clutching his prize: the sea-green Element Gem.

Dragon was sitting on a rock where Tom had left him. He stood up as Tom came limping down the hill.

"You won," Dragon said. He sounded satisfied.

Tom nodded.

"You've got the gem?"

Tom nodded again.

"May I see it?"

Tom held up the Element Gem to show Dragon.

Dragon reached for it.

Tom snatched his hand back.

Dragon frowned.

"What's this?" he said. "I asked to see the gem."

"And now you've seen it," Tom said. He closed his fist around the Element Gem, hiding it from view.

"I want to hold it," Dragon insisted.

"Why?" said Tom. The pain from his face was beginning to die down. It still hurt to talk, but not as badly now. He could move his mouth again. And Tom *had* to have this conversation.

"Why not?" said Dragon. "Let me hold it."

"Dragon," Tom said, "my face is all messed up. You can see that. I'm sure one of my ribs is broken. You can probably tell that from the way I'm holding my arm round my chest. I must look like someone's driven a ten-ton truck over me. But have you asked if I'm OK? Have you offered to help me? No."

Tom's eyes narrowed.

"What you care about is the bloody Element Gem," he went on. "And that's all you care about. And I'm asking myself, why is that?"

Dragon was angry, but tried to stay calm.

"I'm sorry, Tom," he said. "I wasn't thinking. It's clear you're in a bit of pain."

"A *bit* of pain!" snorted Tom.

"But I'm simply keen to make sure that the gem is safe," Dragon said.

"It's safe," said Tom. "I've got it in my hand. It's as safe as it can be."

"Still," said Dragon, "I'd like to hold it. To ... to have a proper look at it."

"Say please," said Tom.

Dragon clenched his teeth. "Give me the Element Gem, Tom."

"You didn't say please."

"Give it to me!" Dragon barked. "Now!"

He took a step towards Tom.

Tom took a step back.

"Who are you, Dragon?" he asked. "I said I wanted to carry on our little chat. So let's do that. Who are you really?"

"I'm not sure if you really want to know the answer to that, Tom."

"Trust me, I do. Because," Tom said, "I know you've been my *sensei*. I know you've been training me to fight the Lords of Pain. But I'm getting the feeling that you're not really on my side."

"The gem, Tom," said Dragon. His voice was low. Menacing. He held out his hand. "Just give it to me. You'll save yourself a great deal of trouble if you do as I ask."

"You see, I've been thinking," said Tom. "I've been thinking about the last three duels, or rather what happened *after* the last three duels. The first time, I handed you the Lord of the Mountain's Element Gem after I dug it out of him. You took it, stuck it in your pocket, then gave it to my mum when we got back to the car park. The second time you got the Lord of the Void's gem off me while I was passed out. I never saw it till later, when Mum had it. The third time, with the Lord of Tears, I gave his gem to you. You gave it back to me almost at once."

"What's your point, Tom?"

"I think you know what I'm getting at. Each time, you had the gem for a little while, Dragon. Not long. But long enough to do something with it."

"Something? Such as?"

"That's what I haven't worked out yet," said Tom. "I didn't suspect that there was anything funny going on at the time. Why would I? I trusted you. You're Dragon. You've done nothing but help me for seven years. Why shouldn't I hand you the Element Gems? But the way you've been acting lately – it's started to make me wonder. And now, right now, you would do anything to get hold of this gem."

Tom waved his hand in the air.

"You can't wait to get your paws on it," he went on. "And if I let you have it, what's the betting it goes in your pocket, then comes out again a short while later? Only, maybe ..."

Tom's voice trailed off. A thought had struck him.

Yes, that was it. That explained it all. That would make sense.

"Maybe," he said, "the gem that comes out of your pocket isn't the same one that went in."

He looked at Dragon's face.

Dragon stared back at him. His face was blank. But ... was there a slight smile on those lips of his? A gleam in those orange-brown eyes that told Tom that his guess was correct?

"Am I right?" said Tom. "I am, aren't I?"

Dragon said nothing. But then, slowly, he began to nod.

"Well worked out, Tom," he said. "It took you a while, but you got there in the end. Seems there is a brain somewhere inside that thick skull of yours after all. Junk food and video games haven't completely rotted it away."

"It was like some magic trick," Tom said. "A very basic one. You switched the real Element Gems with fake ones that were already in your pocket. You replaced them with look-alikes."

"It was easy to do, yes," said Dragon. "*Elementary* stuff, if you'll pardon the pun."

"But I still can't work out why. Why would you collect the gems? What good are they to you? They belong with the Yamada family. They're ours to look after till the next Contest."

"There isn't going to be a 'next Contest', Tom," Dragon said.

"Of course there is. I'll take down the Lord of Fire, two months from now. Then it's all over. The world's safe for another 30 years."

"You are so confident," said Dragon. He made a tut-tut sound. "And so wrong."

"It's quite clear that I'll have to do it without your help," Tom said. "You can't be my trainer any more. Not after this. But I'll manage. I'll get Mai to help me. She'll know the names of a few martial arts experts. Maybe she'll even train me herself."

"You're not hearing what I am saying, Tom," said Dragon. "The Contest is over. Everything's over. You lost. Now, one last time ..." The golden flecks in Dragon's eyes were swirling. Glittering. As if a strong wind inside him was scattering them round in circles. "Give. Me. The. Element. Gem."

"Come and get it," Tom replied. "Take it off me."

"You think you could stop me?" Dragon sneered. "In the state you're in? I could grab that gem off you in a moment, even if you were in top form. I just want to do this in as gentle a way as possible. I don't want to cause any more harm than I have to."

"How kind of you," said a sarcastic Tom. "I thought you didn't like me any more. But you must do, if you still want to be 'gentle' with me."

"Don't push me, boy," said Dragon. "I need that gem. I will have that gem. You can give it up of your own free will, or I will take it by force."

"The easy way or the hard way, huh?" said Tom. "OK. Well, whatever you want the gem for, I'm not handing it over to you without a fight. I'm a Yamada. It's my duty to protect the Element Gems. So ..."

Tom reached for his *katana*.

"The hard way," he said.

Dragon sighed and shook his head, like a teacher dealing with a very dense pupil.

Tom was able to pull the *katana* just a couple of inches out of its sheath. Next thing he knew, he was flat on the ground. Dragon had dropped into a crouch and swiped Tom's legs out from under him with a low roundhouse kick.

Tom landed on his chest, on the side where the broken rib was. The pain was like nothing on Earth. Everything seemed to go white, as if a million-watt flashbulb had lit up in his brain.

He felt fingers clawing at his hand. Dragon, trying to get at the Element Gem.

Tom clenched his hand as tightly as he could. Dragon would not have the gem. He would not.

Dragon began to prise Tom's fingers from around the gem. Tom let out a cry that was half growl, half scream. He reached for one of his weapons with his free hand. Any weapon would do. He pulled the *chigiriki* out from his belt.

Dragon swatted the *chigiriki* out of Tom's grasp before Tom could even try to use it.

Tom felt the fingers of his other hand being bent back. He felt them creaking with the strain.

"No-o-o!" he yelled.

But it was no good. Dragon forced Tom's fingers back ...

Back ...

Further back ...

Crack!

Tom's index finger was pushed back so far, it broke.

Tom howled with the pain. He couldn't keep a grip on the Element Gem any more. He felt Dragon tug it free from his grasp.

Dragon stood up.

His face was a mask of triumph.

"Mine!" he cried. "Mine at last!"

Chapter 12
The Fifth Lord of Pain

Tom rolled onto his back, groaning with pain and despair.

Dragon gazed down at him.

"Don't take it so hard, Tom," he said. He sounded almost kindly – kindly like a vet about to put a sick pet out of its misery. "You never stood a chance. The Element Gem was always going to end up in my hands. It just had to be."

"You – you – " Tom called Dragon the most vile word he knew.

"Come, now," said Dragon. "No call for such language. There's nothing worse than a sore loser. Look on the bright side. You've won four out of five of your duels. That's an incredible feat, not least for one so young. I've no doubt you'd have beaten the Lord of Fire as well, under normal conditions. But the conditions, as I'm sure you know by now, are anything but normal. Tell me, Tom, why do you think the Lords of Pain started the Contest early this time?"

"Don't know," Tom said. "Because they're big fat cheaters?"

"No," said Dragon, speaking as if to a small child. "They started it early because they had to. They had no choice. Everything was not as it ought to be. The terms and conditions of the Contest had already been broken. Something had happened which meant the Lords of Pain weren't able to sit and wait for another fifteen years, till they were at full strength again. They had to act now. They had to make a huge effort and recall their gems early. Do you have any idea what that something might have been?"

"No." Tom made a face as a fresh wave of pain shot through him.

"There's no reason why you should. It goes back to the last Contest. Your father beat all the Five Lords. One of them, however, did not return to the world he had come from, as he should have done. One of them was able to stay on Earth."

Dragon sat down beside Tom. He rolled the Lord of the Typhoon's Element Gem around in the palm of his hand. His voice had taken on the soft tones of someone telling a bedtime story.

"This Lord of Pain was the very first your father fought and defeated," he said. "He lay there in the arena after the duel, in terrible agony. His body was a wreck. His chest had been hacked wide open and his Element Gem taken out. His spirit should have fled back to the demon world, to begin the long, hard process of building up a new body around itself. But this didn't happen. Because this Lord of Pain was angry. He was truly angry. He'd had enough of the cycle of Contest after Contest – of the same thing repeating itself over and over again every 30 years. It had gone on for hundreds of years. The Five Lords fought a Yamada. The Five Lords lost. He was sick and tired of it.

"And so this Lord of Pain decided it was time to change matters. He forced himself to stay alive. He forced his body to heal itself. He crept out of the arena, following in the footsteps of your father, who had already walked away. He dragged himself – yes, dragged – across the ground. It took all of his power to do this – his magical power *and* his will-power. But he did it.

"He made it out of the arena and onto the Earth. Here, he saw at once that he couldn't be a demon any more. He couldn't survive in his current form. He was too weak for that. He was not strong enough to restore his super-charged duel body. That would have needed a lot of magical energy which he no longer had. And so there was nothing else for it. He had to take on a human form.

"Doing that used up the very last of his magic. The Lord of Pain was now, in effect, just a human being. Just a man. A man with the mind and reflexes of a demon, but still only a man. Mortal. Frail. Feeble.

"Remember I told you that the bodies used by the Lords of Pain for the duels are like cars? This Lord of Pain had fought in a body like a Ferrari. Now he was confined to one that was more like a family hatchback.

"But the 'driver' inside was still a demon. An arch-demon, no less. And he had plans. Such plans!"

Dragon chuckled.

"He wanted his Element Gem back, first and foremost," he said. "He needed its power. But he knew he wouldn't be able to get to the gem easily. Kenji Yamada had it, and would protect it with all his might.

"So the Lord of Pain resolved to bide his time. To wait. Perhaps Kenji Yamada would lose one of his next four duels. Then it wouldn't matter. The Lord of Pain would get his gem back anyway.

"But your father won his Contest, of course." Dragon huffed. He sounded really fed up. "So all five Element Gems were with the Yamada family again. And they were guarding them. That was very annoying for the Lord of Pain. And then your father died soon after the Contest was over, and your mother got to look after the gems. Off she went with you, Tom, back to England.

"And the Lord of Pain followed. Followed the two of you to London.

"And waited till the time was ripe.

"The Lord of Pain knew he couldn't get to his Element Gem, or to any of them. It was agony for him. He could hear his gem calling to him. He could hear its voice, like a song, wafting to him across London, faintly. It was somewhere in the city, but he had no idea where. So near, and yet so far. And he knew the gem would be somewhere safe, hard to reach, somewhere where he couldn't possibly get to it …

"Unless, perhaps, he somehow got close to Jane Yamada and her son. Unless he made friends with Mrs Yamada and became something like a father to the son. And he hit on a brilliant means of doing this.

"He would become Tom Yamada's martial arts trainer!"

Dragon laughed.

"What irony!" he said. "A Contest champion, being trained by his enemy, by one of the five arch-demons he was destined to fight. It was crazy. Mad. But that's how things turned out. Seven years passed. Then the Lord of Pain made his move. He tricked his way into the lives of the champion and his mother. He gained their trust, easily, oh, so easily. It helped that they weren't living in Japan. They'd moved away from the influence of the Yamada clan. They were on their own, wallowing about, helpless, you might even say lost. Then along came this martial arts teacher, who seemed to be just what they were looking for.

"But in truth he wanted only one thing. His Element Gem back. And if he could get hold of the other Element Gems too, that would be a plus. Then he would have his own power *and* the power of the other four Lords of Pain. He would have all their magic put together. He would be the arch-demon of all arch-demons!

He would have power over the other four Lords. He would rule them and all the other demons. Anything he wanted would be his.

"You know who I am now, don't you, Tom?" Dragon finished. "Have I answered your question at last?"

"The Lord of Fire," Tom croaked.

"The Lord of Fire! Yes!" Dragon said with pride. "The clue was there all along, but you were too blind to see it. My name. Dragon. A beast from old legends always linked with fire. A beast that lives in fire. That breathes fire."

"And your eyes," said Tom. "In Tokyo. I saw them … burn."

"Yes. I thought you might have done," said Dragon. "I lost my temper. Lost control. My inner demon showed itself. When I'm in true demon form, my eyes glow red, like those of the other four Lords. In this human form, my eyes are these orange-brown ones you see, with the golden flecks inside. But the fire in me comes out in them, if I'm not careful. That day in Tokyo, I was not careful. But my mistake did not tip you off as to who I really was. My true identity was still my secret."

"Great-aunt Akiko," Tom said. "She knew about you. Knew there was something wrong about you. Spotted it the moment she saw you."

"But couldn't work out what it was," said Dragon. "Silly woman. Nowhere near as skilled a witch as she thinks. Still, I'll fix her. When the Earth is mine, Akiko Umari will get what's coming to her. I have plans for her. I'll show her why we're the Lords of Pain."

"When the Earth is ...?"

"Come on, Tom!" Dragon raised his eyebrows. "Don't you understand? It's quite clear, isn't it? What else have we Lords of Pain been trying to get at, for all these hundreds of years? What is it that we've wanted, above all else? Your world. And now I can have it all to myself. I don't need the other four, not any more. I have their gems. I alone will lead the demon armies and come to claim this planet for myself. I alone will be Earth's supreme ruler!"

His eyes blazed all of a sudden. Flames danced in the pupils. They were windows into hell.

"It's going to be fun, Tom. Such fun," he said.

Tom said something. His voice had shrunk to a faint rasp. He hardly heard his own words.

"Speak up, Tom," said Dragon. "What was that?"

Tom said it again, just loud enough this time. "I'll kill you."

"Kill me?" said Dragon. "I think not. No."

"I will. In the next duel. The final one."

"Tom, Tom, Tom," said Dragon, shaking his head, full of pity. "Do you still not get it? There isn't going to be a final duel."

"Yes, there is. The legend. The gods have ordered it. The Five Lords of Pain can take over the Earth only if they win a Contest. That means winning all five duels. You haven't. Yet."

"Tom, the Contest is no more. That whole rule-ridden code has gone. We don't have to follow that any longer."

"We do. You're bound by the bargain you made with Yoshiro Yamada, whether you like it or not. You can't have the Earth unless it's over my dead body."

"Over your dead body?" said Dragon. "We can see to that. I can sort that out right now, on this very spot. With a single blow."

"No, it has to be in fair combat."

Dragon scowled at Tom. His lips curled.

Then his face smoothed out. His expression became calm again, in-control.

"I suppose," he said, "that you might have a point. There is a certain – what's the word? A certain matter of playing by the rules here. It wouldn't be right if I didn't do things in the proper way. Very well, Tom. You can have your duel with me. Two months from now. I've waited this long. I can wait a little longer.

"But remember," Dragon went on. "I'm only agreeing to this because it amuses me to do so. Amuses me, because you don't have a hope of defeating me. Not a chance. Not a prayer. You'd be insane to think you might. I taught you. I trained you. You don't have a single move that wasn't shown to you by me. And I will build myself a duel body like never before. With four Element Gems, I can make it stronger and more powerful than any duel body there's ever been. You can't win, Tom.

Simple as that. You. Can't. Win. Do you understand?"

Tom moved his head slightly.

"Is that a yes or a no, Tom?"

"It's a go-shove-it-where-the-sun-doesn't-shine, Dragon."

Dragon grinned, showing all his pointed little teeth. "Oh, that fighting spirit of yours. That *kiai*. You have so much of it. But it won't get you anywhere, Tom – except dead."

Dragon stood.

"Goodbye, Tom. I'll go down the hill and tell your mother where to find you. She'll come and help you. And then you and I will see each other again in October. I look forward to it. Very much. It'll be a pleasant get together – although I doubt it'll last very long."

Dragon walked off. Tom heard his footsteps, crunching over the burnt ground.

Tom lay there, staring up at the sky. He could feel the blood drying on his cheek, the wound sealing itself. He could feel his broken rib and finger, sending their distress signals jangling along his nerves to his brain. He could feel the heat of the earth beneath him, and it made him think of the fires that had swept across the island two days ago and the fire that might be coming two months from now.

A fire that would consume the whole world.

The fury of the Lord of Fire.

Only he, Tom Yamada, could prevent it.

And he would try. God knows, he would try.

But he didn't believe for one moment that he would succeed.

List of Japanese Words

Akiko: female name; it means either "autumn child" or "bright child"

Dojo: a school which trains in the arts of one-to-one combat (martial arts)

Gi *(say it with a hard g, like in 'go')*: martial arts uniform. Loose trousers and a jacket tied at the waist with a cloth belt

Kanji: Japanese writing

Kata: pattern of movements used for learning and practising martial arts

Katana: long sword used by warriors, such as the samurai (see picture)

Kiai *(key-eye)*: fighting spirit

Mai: female name; it means "dance"

Nunchaku: two short pieces of wood joined by a chain

Ohayo: "good morning" in Japanese

Sai *(sigh)*: dagger with prongs on either side (see picture)

Sensei *(sen-say)*: polite name for a master or teacher

Shinobi: another word for ninja

Shuriken: a throwing-star made of iron (see picture)

Check out Tom's final duel in ...

The Lord of Fire

The final duel

Tom faces the Lord of Fire — the most powerful demon of them all. If he loses, the world will *burn* ...

Turn the page to read the start of the next book!

Scars

Tom brushed his teeth, scowling into the bathroom mirror.

The face that scowled back at him was not the face he'd been used to seeing. Not any more.

One side of it was horribly scarred. The scars crossed Tom's cheek in three jagged lines which ran from his ear to the corner of his mouth, thick and red and ugly. They twisted up the whole of that side of his face. The sight of them made Tom feel sick inside. He wanted to close his eyes and pretend the scars weren't there.

But he forced himself to keep on looking at them.

The more he looked, the angrier he got. And the angrier he got, the less he was afraid.

Tom had a lot to be afraid of.

There was less than a week to go till his duel with the Lord of Fire.

Less than a week to go till the end of the world.

Tom told himself not to think that way. He could still defeat the Lord of Fire. He could still win the Contest.

Yeah, right.

Barrington Stoke would like to thank all its readers for commenting on the manuscript before publication and in particular:

Lizzie Alder
Lee Baxter
Richard Brant
Polly Byrne
Josh Caddy
Andrew Campbell
Mary Campbell
Sean Campbell
John Cowe
Ryan Crowle
Billy Elliot
Brandan Ellis
George Evans
Ronnie Forsythe

Jake Francis
Robert Garside
Susan Gillespie
CJ Lethbridge
Chris McClury
Nathan Morgan
Thomas Pearman
Tré Pusey
Rachael Sargent
Haydn Smallwood
Martisha Thompson
Jordan Truscott
Kim Wherry
James Wright

Become a Consultant!

Would you like to be a consultant? Ask your parent, carer or teacher to contact us at the email address below – we'd love to hear from them! They can also find out more by visiting our website.

schools@barringtonstoke.co.uk
www.barringtonstoke.co.uk